This book belongs to:

A Perfect Little Piglet

Disney's Out & About With Pooh
A Grow and Learn Library

Published by Advance Publishers

Written by Rita Balducci
Illustrated by Arkadia Illustration Ltd.
Designed by Vickey Bolling
Produced by Bumpy Slide Books

ISBN:1-885222-56-4
10 9 8 7 6 5 4 3

One winter afternoon, not long after lunchtime, Piglet found himself hurrying through the Hundred-Acre Wood. He was on his way to Pooh's house for a tea party, and he didn't want to be late.

"Oh, bother," he huffed, wishing his legs were longer. But soon enough he was knocking on Pooh's door.

"Come in!" called Pooh. Standing on his tiptoes, Piglet reached for the doorknob to let himself in.

"Hello, Piglet," Pooh said cheerily. "Have you been running?" Piglet just nodded, trying to catch his breath.

As Piglet made himself comfortable, Pooh carefully set the table.

"Piglet, would you mind taking down the teacups?" Pooh asked as he busied himself with a jar of cookies. "They're in the cupboard right behind you."

Piglet opened the cabinet door, but he didn't see any teacups.

"They're on the top shelf," Pooh said helpfully, spreading honey on a cookie.

Piglet stepped back and looked up. There were the teacups, in a neat row high above his head. Piglet glanced over at Pooh, then back to the teacups. Then he jumped as high as he could, stretching to reach inside the cupboard.

"Are you all right?" Pooh asked, for Piglet had knocked over a stool on the way down.

"No, I'm not, Pooh. I'm too small — too small to run fast and too small to reach teacups," Piglet said sadly. "Folks who are little can't do anything right."

Pooh set Piglet's stool straight, then brought down the cups. "What about bees?" Pooh said thoughtfully.

"Bees?" Piglet repeated.

"Bees are much, much smaller than you are," Pooh said. "And they do something very important. They make honey."

Piglet thought about this as he drank his tea and ate his cookies. Pooh was right, he decided. Bees *were* important.

"But I'm not a bee," Piglet sighed as he walked home. "There's nothing that special about me."

Suddenly a cold wind blew around Piglet, whisking his little hat from his head. Piglet watched it disappear into the woods as snow began to fall softly all around him.

"Yahoo!" boomed Tigger's familiar voice as he bounced out of the trees holding Piglet's hat. "Is this yours, Piglet?"

"Thanks, Tigger," Piglet said, taking back his hat. "I'll be needing this more than ever now. Look, it's snowing!"

"Isn't it great?!" laughed Tigger, bouncing in circles around his friend. "I LOVE SNOW!"

Piglet looked down at his mittens. "Tigger, come look at these snowflakes!" he cried. "They're beautiful!"

Tigger stopped bouncing long enough to take a peek. "Wow!" he said. "That one looks just like a tiny star."

"Let's taste some!" Tigger shouted, catching snowflakes on his tongue.

Piglet opened his mouth and started to giggle.

"They tickle!" he squealed.

"Makes me feel like bouncing!" Tigger said as he bounced off into the woods again.

Piglet just stood there, watching the tiny snowflakes as they danced in the air. They were so perfect. "And so very, very small," Piglet whispered to himself.

Piglet continued on his way, wrapping his scarf a little more tightly around his neck. Before long he spied his friend Roo up ahead, looking at something in the snow.

"Oh, Piglet! Come see what I've found!" Roo called out to him.

When Piglet hurried over, he looked where Roo was pointing and saw a small nest.

"The wind must have blown it down," said Piglet.
Together they studied the little nest of twigs and grass.
It was tiny but sturdy, with not a twig out of place.

"It looks so soft and snuggly inside," Roo said. "Just like
Mama's pouch."

"I wonder what kind of bird made it," Piglet said. "It's awfully small."

"I know!" Roo said. "A hummingbird! They're the smallest birds of all!"

Piglet carefully placed the nest in a nearby bush.

"I'm glad we were able to save that hummingbird's home, Roo," he said.

"Me, too," Roo replied. "Now *I've* got to go home. It's nap time!" And with that he was on his way.

Piglet stood before the little nest, picturing how **safe** and warm and cozy it must be for the hummingbird who lived there.

"Hmmm," Piglet thought. "Bees are small. Snowflakes are small. Hummingbirds and their nests are small. Maybe being small isn't so bad, after all. Of course, I still can't reach Pooh's teacups."

And, feeling just a bit better, he began to whistle and skip through the woods.

Piglet might have gone on whistling and skipping if he had not run into Eeyore, who was sitting glumly in the middle of the path.

"Hello, Eeyore!" Piglet called brightly, hoping to cheer up his friend.

"Oh, it's you, Piglet," Eeyore sighed.

"What's the matter?" Piglet asked. "You look even sadder than usual."

Eeyore sighed again. "Look," he commanded, turning slowly in a circle in front of Piglet. "It's happened again."

Piglet looked closely at Eeyore. "Your tail is missing," he guessed, hoping he was right.

Eeyore nodded. "It blew off when the snow began to fall," he explained.

Piglet thought about all the fun he had had catching snowflakes on his tongue, but one look at Eeyore made him decide not to mention it.

"It's under that bush," Eeyore continued. "But every time I try to get it, all the twigs and thorns catch on my ears and scratch my back. I guess this time my tail is gone forever."

"Don't worry, Eeyore," Piglet reassured him. "I will get your tail for you!"

And marching up to the bush, Piglet took a deep breath and crawled underneath.

There was the tail, all right. Piglet stretched out his hand and grabbed it, but before he crawled back out, he looked up through the bush's twisted branches.

Here and there, sunlight glistened on tiny patches of
snow, and there was a delicate cobweb hidden among
the leaves.

"It's a shame no one but me can see how beautiful it is
in here," Piglet thought.

"Here you are, Eeyore!" Piglet announced as he emerged from under the bush. "Good as new!"

"Oh, thank you, Piglet!" Eeyore cried gratefully as Piglet pinned the tail back in place. "How wonderful it must be to be small like you!"

Piglet waved good-bye to Eeyore and continued walking toward home.

"How wonderful it must be to be small! How wonderful it must be to be small!" he repeated over and over to himself.

Later that day, as Piglet sat in his small chair in his small house, a great big smile came across his small face.
"Yes, I do believe it is wonderful to be small, indeed!" he decided at last.